SCOOB

MINI MYS

SKI TRIP TERROR

by John Sazaklis   Illustrated by Dario Brizuela

PICTURE WINDOW BOOKS
a capstone imprint

Published by Picture Window Books, an imprint of Capstone.
1710 Roe Crest Drive
North Mankato, Minnesota 56003
www.capstonepub.com

Library of Congress Cataloging-in-Publication Data
Names: Sazaklis, John, author. | Brizuela, Dario, illustrator.
Title: Ski trip terror / by John Sazaklis ;
illustrated by Dario Brizuela.
Description: North Mankato, Minnesota : Picture Window
Books, an imprint of Capstone, [2021] | Series: Scooby-Doo!
Mini mysteries | Audience: Ages 5-7. | Audience: Grades K-1. |
Summary: "Ready . . . Set . . . Snow! Scooby-Doo and
the Mystery Inc. gang are looking forward to a peaceful
winter vacation. But a sneaky snow ghost is whipping
up a blizzard of trouble! The gang's relaxing ski trip
quickly snowballs into a mystery-solving adventure
in this entertaining early chapter book featuring
Scooby-Doo and his friends"—Provided by publisher.
Identifiers: LCCN 2020036559 (print) | LCCN 2020036560
(ebook) | ISBN 9781515882817 (hardcover) | ISBN
9781515883159 (paperback) | ISBN 9781515892267 (pdf) |
ISBN 9781515893110 (kindle edition)
Subjects: CYAC: Mystery and detective stories. | Skis and
skiing—Fiction. | Ghosts—Fiction. | Great Dane—Fiction. |
Dogs—Fiction.
Classification: LCC PZ7.S27587 Ski 2021 (print) | LCC PZ7.
S27587 (ebook) | DDC [E]—dc23
LC record available at https://lccn.loc.gov/2020036559
LC ebook record available at https://lccn.loc.gov/2020036560

Design Element: Shutterstock: ProStockStudio
Designer: Tracy Davies

TABLE OF CONTENTS

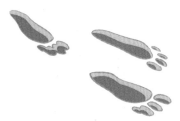

MEET THE MYSTERY INC. GANG!

SHAGGY

Norville "Shaggy" Rogers is a laid-back dude who would rather search for food than clues . . . but he usually finds both!

SCOOBY-DOO

A happy hound with a super snout, Scooby-Doo is the mascot of Mystery Inc. He'll do anything for a Scooby Snack!

FRED

Fred Jones, Jr. is the oldest member of the group. Friendly and fun-loving, he's a good sport—and good at them too.

DAPHNE

Brainy and bold, the fashion-forward Daphne Blake solves mysteries with street smarts and a sense of style.

VELMA

Velma Dinkley is clever and book smart. She may be the youngest member of the team, but she's an old pro at cracking cases.

MYSTERY MACHINE

Not only is this van the gang's main way of getting around, but it is stocked with all the equipment needed for every adventure.

CHAPTER ONE

SNOW DAY

Snowflakes swirled around as the Mystery Inc. gang reached Wolf's End Lodge.

"This ski trip is going to be groovy," Fred said.

"I can't wait to hit the slopes!" said Daphne.

"Like, we can't wait to slurp some hot cocoa!" Shaggy exclaimed.

"Rith rarshmallows!" added Scooby-Doo.

The gang met the resort owner, Mr. Greenway, and some of the other guests.

One of them was a nervous-looking Mr. Leech. He clutched his briefcase close and cried, "Beware the Snow Ghost! He's out there!"

"**ZOINKS!**" said Shaggy. "Did he say g-g-ghost?"

"**RUH-ROH!**" added Scooby-Doo.

"There's no such thing as ghosts," said Mr. Greenway. "Let me show you to your rooms."

Daphne and Velma bunked in one room. Scooby-Doo, Shaggy, and Fred shared another. Shaggy quickly opened his suitcase.

"Like, let's unpack and have a small snack!" Shaggy said.

"This room is stuffy," Fred said. "I'm going to open a window."

He pulled back the curtain to a big surprise—a big, burly beast! ROAR!

"It's the Snow Ghost!" Shaggy screamed.

CHAPTER TWO

COLD CASE

The mysterious monster climbed into the room. Shaggy pulled on the doorknob.

"Let us out! Let us out!" Shaggy, Fred, and Scooby shouted.

Daphne and Velma rushed to the boys' room and pushed on the doorknob.

"Let us in! Let us in!" they shouted.

Suddenly, the door gave way and the teens took a tumble. CRASH!

Then they heard screams from down the hall.

"We've been robbed!"

"Us, too!"

Something suspicious and spooky was going on.

"I warned you about the ghost!" said Mr. Leech.

Just then, Scooby's ears perked up. He pointed in the direction of a strange sound.

"**JEEPERS!**" Daphne shouted. "Look out the window!"

"**JINKIES!**" added Velma. "It's the Snow Ghost!"

"He's not getting away this time!" Fred said.

Scooby and the gang grabbed
their gear and sprang into action.

The Snow Ghost zoomed down
the slope. It looked like he was
flying! When he zigged, the kids
zagged.

They were so close to cracking the case when—**POOF!**—the frosty foe disappeared in a puffy white cloud.

CHAPTER THREE

CHILLY CHASE

"**ZOINKS!**" Shaggy shouted. "Like, we're ghosts too!"

"No, we're not," Velma said. She examined him with her magnifying glass. "It's a mix of powdered sugar, baking soda, and flour."

"Mmmm!" Scooby said as he licked Shaggy clean. "Relicious!"

"Thanks, Scoob!" Shaggy said.

"Check it out, gang!" Fred exclaimed.

There was a trail of large footprints in the snow. The friends followed them until they reached a wall.

"**JEEPERS!**" Daphne said. "It's a dead end!"

"And, like, I'm dead tired," Shaggy said. He leaned against the wall.

Suddenly, the wall flipped around—**WHOOSH!**—to reveal a secret room inside the lodge!

There was Mr. Leech—and his briefcase full of stolen items!

"Aha!" shouted Fred. "Your footprints led us right to you, Leech."

Just then, there was a loud ROAR!

The Snow Ghost appeared and snatched the briefcase. Then the massive monster rushed toward the revolving wall. Mr. Leech was right behind him!

Thinking quickly, Velma grabbed a bucket of water.

SPLASH!

Instantly, the ground froze into a slippery sheet of ice under the feet of the frosty foe.

The Snow Ghost landed on top of Mr. Leech.

SMASH!

Then the monster's mask came off to reveal—Mr. Greenway!

"The creature was just a crook in a costume!" Daphne exclaimed.

Moments later, the police arrived to escort the criminals away.

"Our plans were ruined!" yelled Mr. Leech. "No thanks to you meddling kids!"

"Like, you're welcome!" Shaggy shouted back.

Once the stolen items were returned to their rightful owners, Scooby and the gang were ready to forget their ski trip troubles.

"Hanging around with my pooch and my pals is snow much fun!" Shaggy said.

"SCOOBY-DOOBY-DOO!"

GLOSSARY

burly—large and strong

escort—to travel with and protect

foe—an enemy

meddle—interfere with someone else's business

revolve—to turn or to circle around another object

stuffy—lacking fresh air

suspicious—expressing distrust

AUTHOR

John Sazaklis is a *New York Times* bestselling author with almost 100 children's books under his utility belt! He has also illustrated Spider-Man books, created toys for *MAD* magazine, and written for the BEN 10 animated series. John lives in New York City with his superpowered wife and daughter.

ILLUSTRATOR

Dario Brizuela works traditionally and digitally in many different illustration styles. His work can be found in a wide range of properties, including Star Wars Tales, DC Super Friends, Transformers, Scooby-Doo! Team-Up, DC Super Hero Girls, and more. Brizuela lives in Buenos Aires, Argentina.

TALK ABOUT IT

1. How would you have caught the Snow Ghost?

2. Were you surprised that Mr. Greenway and Mr. Leech were working together? Why or why not?

3. Do you believe in ghosts? Talk about your answer.

WRITE ABOUT IT

1. Make a list of at least three things you would do at a ski village.

2. Pretend you are a member of the Mystery Inc. gang. Write a journal entry about your ski trip adventure!

3. Scooby and Shaggy love snacks. Write about your favorite snack.

Help solve mystery after mystery with Scooby-Doo and the gang!

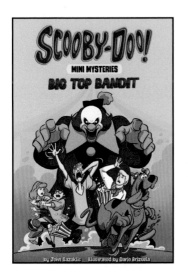

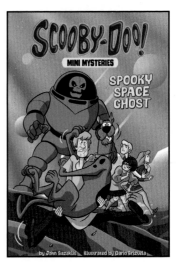

READ THEM ALL!